EDDYCAT
Goes Shopping
with Becky Bunny

For a free color catalog describing Gareth Stevens's list of high-quality books, call 1-800-341-3569 (USA) or 1-800-461-9120 (Canada).

ISBN 0-8368-0947-5

Published by
Gareth Stevens Publishing
1555 North RiverCenter Drive, Suite 201
Milwaukee, Wisconsin 53212, USA

This edition of *Eddycat Goes Shopping with Becky Bunny* was first published in the USA and Canada by Gareth Stevens, Inc., in association with The Children's Etiquette Institute. Text, artwork, characters, design, and format © 1993 by The Children's Etiquette Institute.

Sincere thanks to educators Jody Henderson-Sykes of Grand Avenue Middle School in Milwaukee, Wisconsin, and Mel Ciena of the University of San Francisco for their invaluable help.

EDDYCAT, EddieCat, and the EDDYCAT symbol and Social Skills for Children are trademarks and service marks of the American Etiquette Institute.

Printed in the United States of America

1 2 3 4 5 6 7 8 9 98 97 96 95 94 93

EDDYCAT
Goes Shopping
with Becky Bunny

Gareth Stevens Publishing
MILWAUKEE

CONTENTS

Hi, friends! Remember me? I'm Eddycat, and I live in the city of Mannersville.

Everyone here believes there is something special about certain words and sentences because they make others smile and feel good.

My goal is to try to make the world a better place in which to live, but I need your help. What you need to do is let others know that you care about them and that you care about yourself. I will show you the special way of doing this. And it will make me very happy to cheer you on as you learn to say the special words and follow the special rules!

Summer vacation is over, and Wright Street School starts on Monday. Becky Bunny and Rhonda Rabbit are spending their Saturday before school starts shopping and having lunch together. Mr. Bunny, Becky's father, is taking the two girls shopping at the new grocery store in Mannersville. Would you like to help them shop?

Here are some of the special phrases and magical words used in this Eddycat story. Can **you** find these words and sentences in the story?

Good morning.	*You may.*
May we?	*Please.*
Thank you.	*You're welcome.*

In Mannersville Park, the leaves on the trees are turning lovely shades of red, yellow, and orange. The air has become chilly, and it's the last weekend before the school year begins.

"Oh, it's Saturday!" says Becky Bunny. "Rhonda Rabbit and I are going to help Dad fix lunch. He said we could help him shop for groceries, too!"

"Good morning, Dad," says Becky with a smile. "What time are we going to the grocery store?"

"Good morning, Becky. How about ten o'clock?" asks Becky's dad. "Please call Rhonda and let her know what time we will pick her up."

It's a good idea to make a shopping list before you go to the store so you won't forget anything important.

"Hi, Rhonda, this is Becky Bunny. Is it all right if my dad and I pick you up at ten o'clock?" asks Becky.

"That will be great. I'll be waiting on the steps out front. My mom will watch me from our apartment window to make sure I'm safe," answers Rhonda.

Becky knows it's okay to get dirty when she plays. But she also knows she should be neat and clean when she goes shopping. To get ready, Becky...

1. Showers,

2. combs her hair,

3. brushes her teeth, and

4. cleans her nails.

 "I think I'm ready now!" exclaims Becky with glee.

When Becky and her dad arrive at Rhonda's apartment building, Rhonda is sitting out front as she promised.

The two girls greet each other excitedly and thank each other for being on time.

"My mother taught me to keep my shoes off the car seats," says Rhonda.

"My dad taught me to always wear my seat belt and to make sure my door is always locked," says Becky.

"I also taught you to keep your hands and arms inside the car!" Mr. Bunny reminds them.

It is important to follow the rules in a car so everyone will have a safe and happy ride.

There are so many wonderful things to see and smell in a grocery store. Becky and Rhonda are excited about what to choose for lunch.

"Do you like macaroni and cheese?" asks Becky.

"Oh, I love macaroni and cheese, and I know how to make it, too!" says Rhonda.

It is important to consider what food your guests like when you plan a menu. Becky should be sure to find out what Rhonda likes.

"My mother lets me push a shopping cart by myself because I am very careful," says Rhonda. "I push it slowly and watch where I am going."

"If you run up and down the aisles like a race car driver, someone could get hurt. Or you might knock over a display and cause a lot of damage," says Becky.

"Oh, what beautiful apples!" says Becky.

"We can buy some apples. But we must handle them carefully so that we don't drop any or cause the display to come tumbling down," says Becky's dad.

The grocery clerk works hard to keep the fruits and vegetables from getting bruised, and to keep the display looking nice. We should be careful so that everyone can enjoy the display.

Signs make the store look neat and orderly. They need to stay in place.

"Look at all these wonderful signs," says Rhonda. "Why don't we take them home to play store?"

"My dad likes to buy coffee beans and grind them right in the store," says Becky. "But he told me not to touch the grinder."

Yes, Becky. Machines like this are nice, but they can be very dangerous. Children shouldn't play with them.

"I love ice cream. Let's each get an ice cream bar and eat it right now," says Rhonda excitedly.

When you buy ice cream bars in a grocery store, you must buy the whole box. Pay for the ice cream bars first, and then open the box after you leave the store. Remember, there is no eating in the store unless a clerk has offered you a sample.

"Mr. Bunny, is this where you buy the food for the wonderful snack mix you make?" asks Rhonda.

"Yes, Rhonda. I'm glad you like it. I'll show you how to make some," says Mr. Bunny.

First, remember to carefully scoop out each item with the scoop that is with each bin. Don't use your hands to pick up the food.

Each item goes in a separate bag so that the checker can weigh it and let you know how much it will cost.

Remember. No hands
in the bins!

"Gee, look at all these books and magazines and toys!" says Becky.

It is all right to look through a book quickly to see if you may want to buy it. It is *not* all right to read the book all the way through and then put it back.

If you break the boxes or tear the paper on the toys, the store can no longer sell them. Be very careful, and try to handle only the toys you are going to buy.

"Oh, what fun! They even have a bakery in this store," says Rhonda, rubbing her tummy.

"I remembered that Becky said you like sour dough rolls," says Mr. Bunny to Rhonda, "so I picked some up for our lunch."

"Would you like to try a sample of our cookies?" asks the bakery clerk. The girls get permission from Mr. Bunny before they try a sample.

"Yes, please," says Becky with a smile.

"Thank you," says everyone.

"Oh, Becky, look at the little bell. It looks like the door bell that is in my apartment building," says Rhonda.

Becky notices a special white bag that her dad has placed in the grocery cart. "It looks like we may be getting a surprise from the bakery," whispers Becky to Rhonda.

Sometimes it is hard to wait quietly in a long line, but it is important that everyone feels comfortable. So that means no pushing, no shoving, and also none of Becky's famous cartwheels!

"Oh look, a shirt with my name on it. May we look at them, Dad?" asks Becky.

"Yes, you may look," replies Mr. Bunny. "But I've explained why kids shouldn't wear shirts or anything with their names on them."

"If we have our names on our clothes, strangers could call out our names and fool us into thinking we know them," says Becky.

"Mmmmmmm," says Becky peeking into the bakery bag on the way home. "This looks good."

"May I please turn on the radio?" asks Rhonda.

It's hard to eat in the car and not make a mess. Whenever possible, wait until you get home to eat.

The courteous thing to do is ask if you may turn on the radio or change the station.

"Of course, Rhonda, but please play it softly," answers Mr. Bunny. "Remember, I have to see and **hear** everything that is going on outside while I am driving."

Back at home, the girls and Mr. Bunny make their lunch and eat.

"This is a great lunch," says Mr. Bunny.   "Thank you for helping make it!"

"You're welcome, and thank you, Mr. Bunny, for inviting me and for teaching me how to make the snack mix," says Rhonda happily.

It is fun to help and teach others when those magical words, "thank you," are used.

"Thank you, girls, for helping clean up the kitchen," says Mr. Bunny. "It is great to have such cheerful helpers."

"It's fun to clean up when you can share the work with a friend," says Becky.

When everyone pitches in to help, the work gets done quickly. It makes everyone feel good to help.

Mr. Bunny and Becky take Rhonda home. As Rhonda leaves her friends, she says, "Thank you again. I really enjoyed shopping and lunch!"

"You're welcome, Rhonda. We had a good time, too! Good-bye, see you on Monday when school starts!" says Becky.

It is hard to see such a nice day come to an end. Remember, it is always pleasant to hear others tell us what a good time they had. Do you remember to thank someone when you have a wonderful time?

EDDYCAT'S HELPFUL TERMS

cleanliness
Being sure that you are clean and neatly dressed. Store owners appreciate it when their customers are clean and neat while shopping.

cooperation
Working together to get something done.

manners
Special words and rules used by people that make everyone involved feel more comfortable.

samples
Sometimes grocery stores set out trays with samples of foods they are selling for shoppers to taste. Be sure to ask permission from the adult you are with before taking a sample. And remember, take only one so there will be enough for the other shoppers.

seat belts
Special straps built into cars to keep passengers safe as they travel. In many states, it is against the law to be in a car without wearing a seat belt. Regardless, it is a good habit to buckle up as soon as you get into a car.

"Thank you."
A polite way to let someone know that you appreciate something he or she has given you or done for you.

"You're welcome."
A polite way to respond when someone thanks you.

MORE BOOKS TO READ

Eddycat titles are the authoritative collection on children's etiquette. Nonetheless, the additional titles by other authors listed here represent good support for the concept that courtesy and manners are valuable skills and habits.

Nonfiction:
Eddycat and Buddy Entertain a Guest. Barnett, Manquen, Rapaport (Gareth Stevens)
Eddycat Attends Sunshine's Birthday Party. Barnett, Manquen, Rapaport (Gareth Stevens)
Eddycat Helps Sunshine Plan Her Party. Barnett, Manquen, Rapaport (Gareth Stevens)
Eddycat Introduces...Mannersville. Barnett, Manquen, Rapaport (Gareth Stevens)
Eddycat Teaches Telephone Skills. Barnett, Manquen, Rapaport (Gareth Stevens)

Good Manners for Girls and Boys. Hickman (Crown)
The Muppet Guide to Magnificent Manners. Howe (Random)
Thingumajig Book of Do's and Don'ts. Keller (Childrens)
What to Do When Your Mom or Dad Says..."Behave in Public!" Berry (Living Skills)

Fiction:
Dinner at Alberta's. Hoban (Harper)

PLACE TO WRITE

For more information about etiquette, write to the American Etiquette Institute, P.O. Box 700508, San Jose, CA 95170.

PARENT/TEACHER GUIDE

books   page 18
   Children should be reminded to be careful when browsing through a book or magazine in a store. If the pages become bent or torn, no one will want to buy the book or magazine.

car seating
   When a car is equipped with three seat belts in the front, children should always get permission if two of them want to sit in the front together. Some drivers feel uncomfortable and crowded if more than one person sits in front with them.

cooking   page 25
   Parental supervision is a must when a child is cooking.

names   page 23
   Most awareness programs for children's safety suggest that no names be visible on clothing, lunch boxes or bags, or book bags so that strangers are not able to appear as friends.

punctuality   page 10
   Being on time shows consideration for others. It is a good habit to have beginning at an early age.

service tickets   page 21
   Some stores issue numbered service tickets for customers waiting in line. Children should be taught that these numbers are not to be played with like a toy.

shopping carts   page 13
   Before a child is allowed to wheel a shopping cart through a store, he or she should be old enough to have demonstrated a

sense of responsibility. Children should not be allowed to simply play with a shopping cart or run randomly through the store with it, irritating and endangering other shoppers.

shopping rules

A shopping trip is more enjoyable for everyone if rules are established before leaving home. For instance, you could decide in advance on the type of purchase children will be allowed to make, such as candy, gum, a book, or a sweater. You could decide in advance on the amount of money the children are allowed to spend, such as twenty-five cents for a treat or five dollars for a gift. It is also a good idea to decide in advance where the people in the group should meet if any of them becomes separated from the group.

strangers   page 23

Use every precaution to insure the safety of children by teaching them to not talk to strangers. Try to arrange with your local police department to have an officer speak at your school or day care center about safety rules regarding children.

INDEX